THE
SPHINX
AT DAWN

THE SPHINX AT DAWN

Two Stories

MADELEINE L'ENGLE

OPEN ROAD

INTEGRATED MEDIA

NEW YORK

Copyright © 1982 by Crosswicks, Ltd.

Cover design by Connie Gabbert

ISBN: 978-1-5040-4943-6

This edition published in 2018 by Open Road Integrated Media, Inc.
180 Maiden Lane
New York, NY 10038
www.openroadmedia.com

CONTENTS

PAKKO'S CAMEL

The treasure was kept in a corner at the back of the house where they were staying in Egypt. The boy's father had made a small cupboard, and then a coffer with a cunningly-devised latch; he showed his wife how to open it, and his son, when the child was old enough to ask.

"But what is it, Father?"

"It is yours, my son."

The child picked up a little of the gold and held it wonderingly in the palm of his hand. "Mine?"

"When you were very small it was given to you."

"But Father, who would give me all this?"

"Three men, three strangers from far away."

"But why, Father? We aren't the kind of people who have gold and precious stones. The three men—do I remember them? I'm not sure. I think—"

"You were only a baby, Yehoshuah. They were—" the father hesitated—"they were passing by the place where we were staying at that time, and they saw you in your mother's lap. They stayed with us for the day, and when they left, they gave you all of the gifts that you see in this box. They told your mother and me that one day you might have need of them."

The child looked at his father; the man's direct brown eyes were not returning the gaze, but were cast down at the coffer; the set of the generous mouth was troubled. The boy let the gold slip from his fingers back into the coffer.

When he was a little older he sometimes opened the door of the cupboard and looked questioningly at the coffer; but he did not open it, and he did not ask either his mother or his father about it again. Something about the box disturbed him, and he felt instinctively that his parents would like it to be out of mind as well as out of sight.

Every month or so his mother opened the cupboard to brush away the cobwebs. Once he came upon her sitting there, a wisp of cobweb against the gloss of her hair, looking at the coffer. She did not notice him until he said, "Mother," and then she jumped as though he had called her back from a long distance. She turned and gave him the same far look with which she had been regarding the coffer.

He met her gaze, and when she turned away, shutting the door of the cupboard, he asked for some bread and cheese.

She prepared it for him, wrapping it in a cool, damp linen cloth. "Where are you going?"

"To play."

"In the village?"

"I thought I would go to the desert."

"The sun is very hot, my son."

"I will cover my head. If Pakko will let me ride his camel, I will go to the oasis."

Pakko, as Pa-Khura was called, was the son of the rich man of the village, a camel breeder. Like many rich men, he was not known for his generosity, even to his own family. Pakko's camel was a beast eminently unsellable. One of his ears had almost been ripped off in a fight with another camel. Pakko's camel had been the loser; as a result, he creaked at the joints, needed large quantities of water daily, was cross-eyed and half deaf. His temper had a low boiling point, and he had to be kept separated from the other beasts. He delighted in letting Pakko ride him into the desert, and then he would start to gallop in a manner extraordinary for one so battered. Pakko would shriek at him to stop, jerking violently at the reins, but the camel's mouth was hard and dark as iron. When he had attained maximum speed he would push his forepaws into the sand, spurting dust, and sending Pakko flying over his head.

Pakko hated his camel, but was forced by his father to feed, water, and exercise it. When he could persuade or bully any of his friends to do the job for him, he pretended that he was bestowing a great favour.

Pakko's father was fat and noisy; Pakko was skinny and short of speech, but had the same tiny eyes, green and sharp as cactus thorns, peering out from under a bulging, bumpy brow. His eyes darted here, there, everywhere: he was the only boy in the village to know about the cupboard and the coffer.

He had come, one day, looking for someone to play with; like the camel, he was quarrelsome, and had fallen out with the boys in the compound. He had come to the small white clay house of the foreigners, pretending to himself that he was bestowing the favour of his presence on Yehoshuah; he did not let himself remember that Yehoshuah was always welcome in the games played by the other boys—"Play with me, Yos; come be on our side, Yos." Shrugging, Pakko slouched into the house, without knocking or announcing his presence, because this was the way he did things, hoping to discover something he could put to use one way or another. And so he happened to see Yehoshuah squatting before the open cupboard.

"What are you doing, Yos?" Pakko asked.

The boy did not jump, but turned around slowly and smiled in greeting.

"What's that?" Pakko pointed.

"A coffer my father made."

"Why?"

"It is his trade." Yos looked at his own hands, strong and calloused from using saw, plane, hammer. He, too, could make a coffer, a table, help build a house.

Pakko squatted beside him. "Can I see?"

With no visible show of reluctance, Yos pulled the coffer out of the cupboard. It had recently been dusted. At the back of the cupboard a small spider was busily spinning a new web. "That's right," Yos said, "spin away. Do you like making new lace every month after my mother has cleaned?"

"How does it open?" Pakko asked.

"With that latch."

Pakko fumbled with it. His fingers, though thin, were short and undexterous. He had trouble fastening the camel straps, adjusting the harness. He got impatient now, with the latch.

"If you're rough with it," Yos said, "you'll just break it. Here. This way."

"Well, leave it open, then! Why did you close it again?"

"I thought you'd like to open it yourself."

Pakko shrugged. "I just want to see what's inside."

Yos looked at him, said slowly, "If I show you, will you let it be a secret, something just between you and me?"

"Why? Haven't the other boys seen it? I'm always the last one to be told anything."

"No one else has seen it."

"Why not?"

"It didn't seem important to show anyone."

Pakko scowled. "It's not important, so Pakko can see it, is that it? If it were something important, you wouldn't let me in on it."

Yos sighed, then pealed with laughter. "You're just like your camel. Come, Pakko, it's a joke, I'm very fond of the camel. Let's not fight, you know I'm stronger than you are. Look, I'll open the box for you."

"I don't care if you do or not." But Pakko wriggled closer as Yos's long fingers manipulated the latch. When the lid was raised, Pakko peered in. A ray of sunlight stretched across the room and glinted against the gold, was refracted from the prisms of a crystal bottle. "What's all that?"

"Gold."

Pakko's hand reached towards it, pulled back. "What would your parents be doing with gold? They were very poor when you first came here. My father told me."

Yos said, "My father is a fine carpenter. He'll never want for work, no matter where we are."

"Taking work away from people who've always lived here." Pakko reached into the box and picked up a piece of gold. "Did he earn this honestly?"

For a moment Yos stiffened. Then he laughed. "No wonder you get so many bloody noses and black eyes. You almost got one from me. But I don't need to defend my father. Everybody knows he's an honourable man. Why did you want to anger me?"

Pakko looked surprised. "I didn't. Things just come out of my mouth. I don't mean them."

Yos laughed again. "Just like your camel." His smile was so friendly that Pakko did not take offence. "The gold is mine," Yos said. "All that is in the box is mine."

"Yours? Ha. How would a little boy like you, a carpenter's son, have things like that? I'm two years older than you are, and my father's the rich man of the village, and I don't have pieces of gold, and oil in crystal bottles, and—what's that?—jewelled boxes of incense   are those things bits of glass?"

"I think," Yos said, "that they are rubies."

Pakko sat back on his heels, the jewelled box in his hand. "We all know you can make up stories. All the little kids are after you to tell them stories. But I'm older than you and I know the difference between stories and what's real. How would you get a box with rubies? And I suppose those things are emeralds?"

"It's likely."

"As though it didn't matter! Where did you get all this—stuff?"

"When I was a baby, three men came to the village where I was born, and left it for me."

"Just happened to pass by and leave it, eh? I suppose they were noble princes from foreign lands leaving gifts for the little lord? That's the kind of fairy tale you're likely to tell."

Yos smiled. "They were very wise men. They could read the stories in the stars, and their camels were white as snow in the moonlight, and their robes were velvet and gold. They saw me in my mother's lap, and they left gifts. Perhaps one day, when I'm grown up, I'll have need of them."

"The gold you can spend, the jewels you can sell, and I suppose you could get a few coins for that crystal bottle."

Yos shivered, although it was very hot in the low-ceilinged room. "Let's go ride the camel to the oasis. Some coconut milk would taste good this afternoon."

Pakko returned the jewelled box reluctantly to the coffer. "None of it's real. I know that. But it's pretty. Can I see it again?"

Yos neither argued nor answered the question. "I'll saddle the camel, if you like."

"I can do it perfectly well myself."

"Of course. But don't you like to have someone do it for you? We can pretend you are a great man—"

"Like my father."

Yos locked the coffer and shut it back in the cupboard; a shadow hid his expression. "You have thousands and thousands of camels, and I'm your servant."

"I'll play that," Pakko said.

Instead of shouting at the camel as Pakko did, Yos talked to him, a murmuring humming, and fondled the torn ear, gently, not to hurt. "Now, Pakko's camel, roll over and let me get the strap under your belly, gentle, there's no need to kick, that's it, that's just right, you're a superb camel, the most intelligent camel I've ever known. That's a beautiful smile, Pakko's camel; no human boy's mouth can possibly stretch that wide. If I pulled my lips back that way I'd make you laugh. Do you like coconut milk? If you don't toss us off your back, I'll give you a whole coconut all for yourself. And here's some water to start out with. You're the thirstiest camel I ever knew. What would you do if you had to travel all the way across the desert? You could do it, if you had to. It's just knowing inside yourself that you can be thirsty for a long time if it's necessary."

Pakko, as time went on, got lazier and lazier about exercising his camel, and began to relax into the role of rich merchant, with Yos his servant. The camel relaxed, too, enjoying his almost daily rides into the desert with Yos, because the boy was always consistent with him, never shouting or kicking even on the days when the camel's bones ached, and when folding his legs under him was so painful that he almost jounced his rider off his back. He learned to spend a whole day in the desert without water or complaint. He also began to balk when anyone else came near him.

There came a day when somebody called him Yos's camel, and Pakko was so furious that he wouldn't allow Yos near him for a week. During that time the camel kicked and bit at anyone who came near, and swore at Pakko with great bubblings and snortings.

Yos sought Pakko out.

Pakko shouted, "That beast of a camel! What did you do to him?"

"Nothing. The wind's been blowing the wrong way for his joints, and when it does that he's cross with everybody. But the wind shifted last night and he'll be better today. Let's pretend you're a great prince from a distant land, and I'm your camel boy. I'll saddle him for you, and you can ride all about the village greeting everybody."

"And giving gifts?"

"If you like."

After Pakko had proved publicly to everybody that he could control the camel—no one need know the trouble Yos had gone to before the camel would allow Pakko to mount him—he again let the younger boy resume his care of the beast. When the children referred to Yos's camel, Pakko pretended not to hear, or loftily told them that he graciously permitted Yos to ride the camel as a special treat, because he was a poor foreigner who would never have an opportunity to ride a camel otherwise.

One late afternoon when Yos returned from the desert, he sensed tension the moment he entered the house. His mother and father were waiting for him, their faces grave and troubled.

"Son, where have you been?" his father asked.

"In the desert with Pakko's camel."

"What do you do there?"

"I sit."

The father sighed. "You do your work. I have no complaints. You do not leave until everything is done. But why do you go so often to the desert?"

"The camel needs exercise. And I like the desert. I talk with the animals and birds and I sit and think."

The boy's mother held up her hand. "Yos's going to the desert doesn't necessarily have anything to do with—you know he's always liked to have time by himself."

"To do with what, Mother?"

The mother went to the cupboard in the corner, opened it, and pulled out the coffer. "I dusted today, my son."

"Yes, mother?"

"I do not always open the coffer, but I opened it today."

He stood, looking at her, questioningly. She gazed at him, searched his eyes, then turned to her husband. "You see, he knows nothing."

"My dear," the father said, "he must know."

Yos stood quietly looking from one to the other.

His mother opened the coffer and held it out to him. It was empty. She looked at him, cried out, "He is as surprised as I was!"

Her husband turned away, sat down, and then held his strong, calloused hands out towards the boy. "Yos, my son."

Yos reached towards the hands. "Yes, father."

"What do you know about this?"

"Nothing."

"You did not take the gifts from the box?"

"No, father."

The older man's grip on the boy's hands was strong. "Yos, I trust you. You knew that all that was in the box was yours. If you took it, I know you well enough to know that it was for a purpose which you considered right and necessary. You do not need to tell me what it was."

"But I took nothing, father."

"Yos, nobody knows about the box besides your mother and you."

Yos's eyes were troubled. "One of the boys from the village knows, father."

"You showed him?"

Yos did not try to explain. "Yes, father."

The mother cried out, "But, Yos—"

Her husband withdrew one hand from the boy's, and

held it up to silence his wife. "If Yos wishes to tell us why he showed the coffer to one of his friends, he will do so."

"I wish to tell you, but I can't. At least, not now."

"Can you tell us who it was?"

"No, father."

"My son, you do know what this implies? Someone has taken all that is in the coffer, and if you are not the one who has done so, then it must be your friend."

"Yes."

"There was a great deal of gold in the coffer—"

The mother cried out, "Thirty pieces!"

Again her husband held up a silencing hand. "There were also precious stones, and valuable oil. You see, my son, your mother and I were asked to keep these things for you, and we tried to do so. We want nothing for ourselves. We have all that we need, and for us to have riches would be an embarrassment."

"Then for me, too, father."

"That is not the point. The strangers left the gifts for you."

Yos spoke slowly. "Father, what would you have done if no one had taken the gifts?"

"I don't know, my son, and that is not important. It has always been my experience that when the time comes, then I will know what is to be done. What matters now is that something has happened before that time."

"Father, are you sure?"

"Yos, you are still a child. I understand that you want to protect your friend. But we cannot just shrug off this theft."

For a moment Yos's dark eyes shone with tears. "Oh, no, father, I know that. But—you said that you trust me?"

"I do."

"Let me have some time, first to think what is best to be done, and then to do it."

"Are you old enough to handle such a problem yourself? I think that I must report the loss to the authorities."

"Not yet. Give me—not long; just one day. Till tomorrow night."

"Very well, Yos."

"Tomorrow night look in the cupboard and open the coffer, father. If the gifts are returned, then perhaps we need never mention it?"

"If that is what you wish."

The mother spoke softly, "And what if the gifts are not returned?"

"As my father said, when the time comes, we will know what to do."

"Yos, you are a good boy, a little headstrong sometimes, but always a good boy. Please be careful."

"I will be careful, mother."

His father smiled. "But not too careful. He is a boy."

After his parents were in bed that night, Yos dressed and went to the compound in which Pakko's father kept his camels. He spoke quietly, moving so softly that he barely disturbed the sleeping beasts. There were a few soft bubblings and blowings, but that was all. Except for Pakko's camel, who was laboriously rising to his feet as the boy made his way down the line of stalls.

Yos leaned against him, caressing the torn ear, the mangy-looking fur. "Oh, camel, camel."

The camel's rubbery black lips brushed gently against the boy's neck.

"Pakko's camel, dear camel, I wouldn't disturb you at this hour of night if it weren't urgent. Will you take me out into the desert? Not all the way to the oasis, just a little way, so that I can be where I can think. It will be cool, and you won't get hot and thirsty the way you would under the sun. We will ride slowly. I need to think, Pakko's camel. I need to think." While he spoke he saddled the beast. The camel blew one long, self-pitying stream of bubbles, then peered at the boy from under drooping eyelids with extraordinarily beautiful, long, silky lashes.

"Walk quietly, Pakko's camel, very quietly. We don't want to wake anyone in the village. Hush. Step softly."

There was no moon, and the stars shone, undimmed; the shadow of camel and boy was sharp against the desert sand.

"For you to think," the camel said crossly, "is to do what most people would call to stop thinking."

"My heart is heavy," the boy said. "Thinking is not easy when one is heavy. I thought if I came out to the desert I might be light again."

"Let us hope so. I find this extra weight nearly intolerable. Remember that it takes no more than a straw to break a camel's back. You do know that he stole the treasures, don't you?"

"Stole?"

"You might say that Pakko took them, but that's just playing around with words, and this is no time for that."

"Very well, then, you are right. He stole them. But why? His father gives him everything. And he must have known that I would find out, and that I would know he was the one."

"You assume," the camel said, "that Pakko is capable of thought."

Yos sighed. "It would be easy for me to make excuses for him."

"Easy. And what good would that do him?"

"What must I do, then?"

"Beware of Greeks bearing gifts."

Yos laughed, as the camel had intended. "They weren't Greeks."

"They were foreigners. They might as well have been Greeks, since they weren't Egyptian. Or camel." The animal suddenly capsized onto the sand. Yos was used to these sudden descents, and slid to the ground. He stood, looking up at the lavish carelessness of galaxies flung across the night sky, then lay down on his back on the sand, reaching one hand out to stroke the camel.

"Once upon a time," the camel said, "as I've heard tell, the Greeks came into a village with a camel made out of wood. It was, they said, a gift to the villagers, and everybody admired it extravagantly and with much gratitude. At night a door in the side of the camel opened, and a whole army came out and devoured the village."

Yos laughed again. "The three men who brought me the gifts rode camels, but they were not Greeks, and my father says they were very wise, and knew how to read the stars. I do not understand why they would bring such gifts to an unknown child, but my father says that it was because one day I would have need of them."

The camel rolled over, scratching its flank on the cool night sand. "That day has come, little Yos."

Yos looked at him questioningly.

"The box has been opened, and the gifts have all flown out. What should have been kept shut up in the box is now loose in the world. Greed. Covetousness. Resentment."

Yos continued to stroke the camel's long, dour nose. He closed his eyes, and it seemed that he could feel the sharp, cold light of the stars pricking against his skin.

The camel gave one of his loud and unexpected snorts, then said, "If you would scratch around my left ear it would be helpful. There is something about gifts which you must learn, Yos. They are not only bought for a price by the giver, but those who receive them must pay for them, too."

"But I didn't ask for the gifts!"

"Nobody asks for gifts. They're given. And you have to pay for them. All that gold; all that crystal; all those rubies and emeralds."

"As far as I'm concerned, Pakko can have them."

"And what would happen if you went to Pakko and said, I know you stole my gifts, Pakko, but that's all right, I give them to you?"

"Pakko would hate me, I suppose."

"And himself?"

"He'd hate himself, too."

"Are you going to pay for your gifts by buying hate?"

Yos said, "I think I would like to sit in my mother's lap and cry."

"You're too old for that. You'll be too old for a long time."

"But what am I to do, Camel?"

"If you were a grown-up, you might be able to tell Pakko that you knew what he had done, and that he must put the treasure back, and tell your parents that he was sorry."

"I'm two years younger than Pakko."

"Well, then, how do you suppose Pakko feels right now?"

Yos sat up, held his hands out to the light wind that blew from the stars across the sand. "He's awake, and he feels angry. He's angry with me, because he thinks he's hurt me, and he's angry with himself. And he's telling himself that he really has a right to the treasure because he's the rich man's son and I'm only the son of poor foreigners."

"Now do you understand what I mean about gifts?"

Yos spoke in a loud, pained voice. "Camel, it seems to me that there was death in that box."

"There are two boys I would like you to meet," the camel said. "Close your eyes." Yos obeyed. "Keep your hand on my head. It helps me to think. That's right. Now open your eyes."

Yos looked up, and before him stood a boy who was Pakko, and who was not Pakko: he was not Egyptian, and he was not dressed like an Egyptian. Yos regarded him questioningly.

Pakko-not-Pakko bowed. "I am the son of a great lady from Shunem. She gave much hospitality to Elisha, a man of God."

"I know about Elisha," Yos said. "My father has told me."

"Tell me, then, what he has told you?"

"The Shunammite woman was old, like the wife of our father Abraham, and she had no children. Elisha, the man of God, promised her that in due season she would bear a son, and it happened as he foretold."

"And then?"

"The child went out to the reapers where his father was, and all of a sudden he cried out to his father, 'O my head, my head!' His father told a servant to carry him to his mother; the boy sat on her lap till midday, and then he died. She went up and laid him on the bed of the man of God."

"And you know what happened then?"

"Yes. I know. My father taught me."

"You have been well taught. Elisha, the man of God, brought about two miracles for my mother. The barren conceived, and bare a child. The child died, and was returned to life. I was dead, and then I was alive. What you must know, Yehoshuah, is that these were small miracles, important to the Shunammite woman, my mother, and to me. But they did not make the stars shake in their courses."

Yos felt a coldness touch his limbs. "Why are you telling me this?"

"More is required of you. Much more. I will leave you with my blessing, Yos. It is a small blessing, but it is as strong as the sun because it comes through the man of God."

Yos closed his eyes. The cold of the desert night bit deep into his bones. Close by him he could hear the stertorous breathing of Pakko's camel.

He opened his eyes, and another strange boy was standing in the starlight on the desert sand, Pakko-not-Pakko.

"Yehoshuah," Pakko-not-Pakko said, "I am the son of the widow of Zarephath, a village of Sidon. I fell ill, and my breathing ceased, and Elijah, the man of God, breathed deeply upon me, thrice, and the breath came back to me."

"I have heard much about Elijah from my father," Yos said. "Even more than about Elisha."

"You know, then, perhaps, of the small jar of flour, and the flask of oil, which never failed?"

"My father has told me of them."

"You do not know, I think, that I took flour from the jar, and oil from the flask, in order to get silver for myself?"

"No. That I did not know."

"I was dead, and now I live. That is what Elijah the Tishbite did for me."

The cold bit deeper into Yos. It seemed to chill the very marrow of his bones, the blood in his veins. Again he closed his eyes. When he opened them the pattern of stars in the sky had dipped towards the horizon. The camel was snoring. Yos rose, and his limbs were stiff, as though he had been sleeping in one position for a long time. He touched the camel's long nose gently. The camel gave a loud snore, and twitched his ears.

"Camel," Yos said, "wake up. Wake up. It's almost dawn and we must get back to the village."

Unwillingly the camel lifted one long-lashed lid, closed it again.

Yos continued to stroke his nose. "Camel. Pakko's camel. Wake up. Now."

The camel tried the other eye, batted his lashes delicately, snored.

"Pakko's camel. Now."

Both eyes opened, and the camel blew a stream of noisy, ill-smelling bubbles.

"Camel, what was it all about?"

The camel pulled back his rubbery lips and made his sleepiest neigh.

"Pakko's camel, talk to me, talk to me."

The camel looked at the boy as though he were mad.

"But we did, we talked, and I need to know—"

The camel blew more malodorous bubbles, and rose, creaking, to his knees. He shrugged his bony shoulders: it was obvious, the shrug indicated, that the boy was either out of his mind, or, more likely, since he was usually a sensible boy, had been dreaming.

Nevertheless, Yos felt an enormous wave of affection for the beast and hugged him before climbing into the saddle. The camel moved delicately across the sand. At the edge of the horizon a faint touch of lemon colour separated sand from sky; a low star dwindled, diminished, vanished.

Dawn comes earlier to the desert than the village. When they returned to Pakko's father's compound it was still night, but servants ran to and fro with torches and there was a penetrating, painful sound of wailing.

Yos took the camel quckly to the stable, unsaddled and tended him. One of the camel tenders, with a sickly grin, told him that the place was in an uproar because of the death of the master's son. The boy had been stricken suddenly with a fever during the night, and had expired.

Yos controlled his convulsing shudder. He knew that if he went to the front of the house he would not be allowed in, he, only a boy, a foreigner, a person of no importance. So he went to the back. The servants knew him well and, weeping, told him what had happened.

"He was not," one of them said, "the most pleasant of boys. Nevertheless—"

Yos learned that Pakko was still lying on his bed, and that at this moment only his old nurse was with him.

She looked up and beckoned him to come in. "Your friend is dead," she said, and tears moved quietly down her cheeks. "Not many loved him. But he was the child of my heart, and you, Yos, were his friend."

Yos looked at Pakko. The boy looked thin and white and younger than Yos, and at the same time immeasurably ancient. Yos tried to remember the boys who had come to him in the desert, the boys summoned by Pakko's camel. He remembered, too, small animals he had seen in the desert, small creatures who had been injured and had died before their time. He had often been able to breathe life back into them, to hold his hand over their small bodies until he felt healing, and the blood's rhythm strong once more. Yos spoke slowly, quietly. "I do not think that Pakko is dead."

The nurse hesitated a moment and then said, "I will leave you alone with him."

Yos put his hand on Pakko's chest. It was motionless, silent. He held his hand over the heart. He whispered, "This is what I am asked to do, isn't it?" He felt a pain in his own heart so intense that it crashed across his eyes. But he kept his hand on the cold, still chest. His lips moved: in the desert he often sang to himself the songs of David, and these words came to him now: "In the volume of the book it is written of me, that I should fulfill thy will, O my God: I am content to do it; yea, thy law is within my heart."

—He is like one of those small animals, Pakko is like the lizard who lay scorched on the sand, he is like the night-grey mouse who was bitten by the scorpion, he is like the scorpion who. . . .

Under his hand, Yos could feel Pakko's cold flesh begin to warm. Then there was a small throbbing, like the throbbing in the heart of the small bird Yos had held in his hands for an hour until life came back to it.

Pakko stirred.

Yos closed his eyes. He felt terribly tired.

Pakko woke, and looked startled. "What are you doing here?"

Yos pulled back his hand. Morning light was reaching into the far corners of the room. "I came to ask if you'd like to come spend the day with me, Pakko. It's almost time for my mother to clean the cupboard again, and I thought we might rescue the spiders. And then you could have another look at the treasure, if you like."

Pakko sat up, yawned, covering his mouth and the look of his face with his hand.

Yos said, slowly, "I thought I'd take your camel out for a while first. I'll be back by the middle of the morning, and then I must do some work for my father, so I won't be home until midday. I could meet you here—"

"No," Pakko said, the words hurried. "I'll meet you at your house. I would like to see the treasure again, and I haven't anything better to do today."

The old nurse peered into the room, saw Pakko sitting up, and rushed at him in an ecstasy of joy. Pakko pushed her away crossly. "What's this all about?"

Yos said, "You see he *was* only sleeping," and slipped out of the room.

The camel was snoring, loudly. He had eaten well, had guzzled the water Yos had left for him, and did not wish to be disturbed. Yos said, "It's important. I must go to the desert, Pakko's camel. I need to think."

The camel rolled his eyes. He, being only a camel, did not understand a word that Yos was saying.

But they went to the desert.

The sun was as hot as the starlight had been cold.

"I think," Yos said, "that what Pakko meant when he said that he had nothing better to do, and sounded so grumpy, was that he was happy to be able to put the treasure back, with nobody knowing about it. Has it been paid for now, Pakko's camel? A great miracle is easy to perform. To give life back to a body is no large thing. It is the other death, Pakko's camel, it is the other that is the darkness, and to put light in that darkness is. . . ." He turned to the songs of David again, raising his face and his voice to the vast arc of sky: "For thou wilt light my candle: the Lord my God will enlighten my darkness. Unto thee, O Lord, will I lift up my soul. My God, I have put my trust in thee. I will always give thanks unto the Lord; his praise shall ever be in my mouth. O God, my heart is ready, my heart is ready. I will sing and give praise."

And as he sang, the heavy tiredness left him.

He would have been happy, singing, drinking in the light of the sun, for a long time, but Pakko's camel began nuzzling him, drawing back the black lips, touching them with his tongue, giving every indication that he was about to expire from thirst.

"All right, Pakko's camel. I've worked you hard these past hours, haven't I? We'll go back and I'll draw you a bucket of water."

The camel made noises of gratification; his legs buckled under him, and he waited for Yos to climb into the saddle.

THE SPHINX
AT DAWN

Early morning approached the desert. One by one the stars dimmed, went out. At the crack of dawn on the horizon the light widened to a streak of pale yellow, then warmed to a rosy glow that bathed the sands which stretched and shifted sleepily around the great stone figure of the Sphinx. The stone was touched with light, was softened, quickened, en-fleshed. The enormous wings stirred; the heavy eyelids rose. The Sphinx stared slowly across the desert floor, fixed her hungry gaze on a small speck on the widening horizon.

The speck grew larger, moved closer, was a camel, a white, one-humped camel bearing a rider. At this distance it was impossible to tell the size or tribe of whoever was mounted on the camel's hump; he was simply a small silhouette against the deepening rose of the sky. The cold sands reflected colour, a warm and gentle hue, not the molten brass that would shimmer and burn as the sun ascended.

The camel moved in a steady, rhythmic gallop, rocking like a small boat on a rough sea, coming closer and closer.

The Sphinx waited, her stone lids half closed, then lifted slightly on her leonine forepaws as she saw that the rider was no more than a very young boy. Her long, poisonous tail twitched; her pinions quivered; she lay in her quickened stone, waiting.

At hailing distance the boy raised his arm in greeting.

The Sphinx released a slow, sibilant breath, widened her eyes to stare at him. He waved, smiled, then laughed. As the camel drew up to the great carved beast, the boy slapped the reins gently against the camel's side. The animal's legs crumpled as it dropped its ungainly body to the sand. The boy slid from the hump to the sand and walked up to the Sphinx, gravely regarding the pale, cold eyes.

"Good morning."

"Good morning, young king."

The boy laughed, joyously. "I'm not a king, O Sphinx. But I was told that I would find you here and that we should have a talk before my parents and I leave Egypt."

"Who told you?"

"An old man I met on the highway, a very old man. I should think he was even older than you."

"No one is older than I am, and it is very rude of you to call

me old. I am as young as the dawn. Very well, O Prince, you have come. What do you want of me?"

"I'm not a prince, either. I'm just a boy and my parents are poor."

The camel arched its neck. "Poor but honest."

"And if I had my choice of all the parents in the world, they are the ones I would choose."

"You did," the camel said, and blew three milky bubbles with careful pleasure.

The Sphinx shifted her massive body slightly. *"Why have you come to me, Prince?"*

"But I told you: I'm not a king, nor a prince. I'm just a boy."

"Nonsense. If you are not yet a king, then you are at least a prince. Nobody of lesser degree can see me as you see me, nor hear me as you hear me. I am very hungry. You are far too young for breakfast but a prince hasn't come my way for many generations, so I suppose you will have to do."

The boy opened the saddle bag at the side of the camel and drew out a wineskin and a loaf of bread. "It's not very much, but I'll be glad to share it with you."

"So *kind of you.*"

The camel whinnied to the boy. "Beware. She's up to her tricks again. I warned you not to come."

"Eat your breakfast, little prince. The only way I can share it is by eating you, and I shall be happy to do so. I am hungry for a prince."

The boy broke his loaf and put the largest piece down by the feet of the Sphinx. "I don't think you'd really eat me for breakfast, and this is very good bread. My mother baked it herself. I know that you're not allowed to eat me as long as I can answer your riddles." Without fear he stared at the Sphinx. The Sphinx stared back. The camel blew several more bubbles and then curled his wicked black lips, baring his long yellow teeth, and sneered.

"You are not to tell him the answers," the Sphinx told the camel.

The boy laughed. "Will he have to? I can ask riddles, too, you see, Sphinx."

The Sphinx scowled; she was not pleased with his laughter; he was supposed to be pale with terror. *"I ask the riddles around here."*

The camel nuzzled his leathery lips against the back of the boy's neck, making him laugh at the tickling. "It is not your turn to ask riddles, little son. Later, when you are a man, you will ask riddles. For many people you will, yourself, be a riddle. But you must learn that many things are reversed for you." His long, beautifully-fringed lids dropped over his eyes.

The boy regarded the arrogant beast with affection. "If I can answer the Sphinx's riddles, it is because you have taught me; you never talk in anything but riddles."

"Before you may ask riddles, you must first answer them."

The Sphinx was cross at all the interruptions. She was not used to having anybody else take over the conversation. *"I do not brook any interference, Camel, you know that, so keep out of this. And I do not care for constant interruptions when I am preparing for a pleasant meal. You do understand, don't you, child, that if you cannot answer my riddles I will devour you? The desert is covered with the bones of young princes who have failed to provide me with the correct answers. But I do not fancy eating children. Not enough meat on their bones."*

"I told you I'm not a prince."

"If you are edible you are a prince. You smell delectably edible."

The camel looked impatient. "Stop quibbling. Get along with it."

"Why don't you get along, Camel? Nobody invited you to breakfast."

"I've already eaten, thank you. And I'm not leaving. This is his and my last day together. The young one's years in Egypt are over. The frightened king of his land is dead."

The boy sighed. "I thought perhaps you could explain that, O Sphinx. Why would any king be frightened of me? Can you tell me?"

"You must not ask questions out of turn."

The camel rose, its knobbly knees knocking together. "Let's get this idiotic riddle business over with. She makes me nervous when she's planning breakfast."

"You are not to help him. You must play fair."

The boy looked at the bread he had placed between the cruel paws. "All right. Let's have your riddle."

The Sphinx drew back her claws. *"But is this the time? There was another prince, many years ago, at least twice your age. His feet were pierced and he answered my riddle, but he did the right things at the wrong time, and suffered for it. His name was Oedipus. For all his mistiming he was a king."*

The boy looked down at his feet, tanned and perfect against the lighter tan of the sand. "Kings have come to me, so I'm told, but for all that I am only a boy, an ordinary boy like any other."

The camel made one of its noises and tossed its head.

"Your camel is ill-mannered."

The boy's laugh pealed forth. "Aren't all camels?"

"Why do you like the desert?"

"Is that a riddle?"

"It is a question."

"What is the difference between a question and a riddle?"

"A question may be answered with a lie, but the answer to a riddle must hold truth." Then the Sphinx stopped, furious. *"There! What did I tell you? You're not playing fair! You've made me give an answer! I told you that you are not to ask until you have answered. I'll start off with an easy one. How can there be an eagle without any bones?"*

The child had many friends in the desert, eagles and mice and owls and dragons and ostriches and wild desert asses. He thought now of the eagles and looked up into the pale vault of sky, still untouched by the heat of the sun, but there was no great bird swooping overhead. He regarded the empty sky, imaging an eagle to himself, and then laughed. "That *is* an easy one! An eaglet when it's unhatched, when it's first in the egg, doesn't have any bones."

"*The camel told you!*"

"I didn't say a word."

"*I will not be thwarted so easily.*" The Sphinx's massive tail was twitching back and forth as though to dislodge one of the stinging desert flies which came to plague it. "*In marble walls as white as milk, lined with skin as soft as silk, within a fountain crystal clear, a golden apple doth appear. No doors there are to this stronghold, yet thieves break in and steal the gold.—What is it?*"

The camel tried to stamp with both forepaws at once, stumbled to its knees and then rose with clumsy dignity. "Talk about playing fair—that's much too difficult."

"*I am the Sphinx. I can ask anything I choose.*"

"Within reason."

"*The Sphinx does not have to be reasonable. If I were reasonable I would have starved centuries ago. In any case it follows in absolutely logical progression.*"

"It's mean." The camel curled his nostrils angrily. Then he looked at the child and carefully blew a single bubble.

"The answer is an egg," said the boy.

The Sphinx roared in frustration. *"Who told you?"*

The boy, smiling, looked toward the camel who was rubbing his knees together to relieve their itching. The camel drew his rubbery lips back in a self-satisfied snigger.

"Camels should not be able to answer riddles."

The twitch of the camel's tail matched, in miniature, that of the Sphinx. "Camels listen, and they hear, and they remember. We are ourselves, if not riddles, at least enigmas. There are not many people who know a camel's night thoughts."

The stone tail made a furious clatter. *"Enough. I will ask another riddle. Hush. What walks on four feet in the morning, two feet at noon, and three in the evening?"*

The huge mass of the Sphinx seemed to grow to even greater proportions in the silence.

The boy looked very small as he looked up at the hooded stone eyes. He smiled confidently. "That, O Sphinx, is the question Oedipus answered on his way from Corinth to Thebes. The camel didn't need to help me with that. Everybody in Egypt knows the answer to that riddle."

"Answer it, then."

"Man, O Sphinx, is the answer. At any rate it is the answer which was given by Oedipus and you accepted it:

man, who crawls on all fours as a baby, stands upright as a young man, and walks three-legged with a stick in old age. I really don't think it's a very good riddle and I don't know how you managed to make so many meals over it. Have you really eaten many men, Sphinx?"

"*Many.*"

"Then you are many men, are you not? And if I cannot answer your riddles and you eat me, then you will be me, too."

"*You will learn, child,*" the Sphinx said, "*that we all live by eating of each other. If you eat only my words, you are a part of me.*"

The boy laughed up at the broken stone face. "Do you ever eat your own words?"

"*Never.*"

"And do you really want to eat me?"

"*I am tired of men, child. I would make men kings, and instead I have to digest them inwardly, which is often a fearful nuisance. Or, like Oedipus, they come with a curse, out of joint with time. What is time?*"

"Is that the next riddle?"

"*You may answer it as such.*"

The child closed his eyes thinking. "Time is a thought, in my head and yours. It is a river which changes even as we step into it. It is what holds you here in the desert, imprisoned in stone." He opened his eyes.

Beside him the camel moved his foolish head on the long curved neck back and forth to catch a tiny breeze; his red eyes caught the fiery rays of the sun which was beginning to throw long arms of light up over the horizon.

The Sphinx gave a low, dragon's growl. *"What is more unkind than wind?"*

The child cocked his head at the Sphinx, smiling, thinking, unafraid. The camel rose awkwardly, ambled across the sand, and blew gently in the little boy's ear.

The child laughed. "Ingratitude, Sphinx. Blow, blow, thou winter wind: thou art not so unkind as man's ingratitude."

The Sphinx raised an angry stone paw and banged it down with a crash like thunder. *"I demand an explanation!"*

The camel whickered, rolling its red eyes in satisfaction.

"Oh, I saw you tell him, you ingrate, you proof of the riddle's truth. But how did you know the answer? It's out of your time and sphere entirely."

"Then it wasn't a fair question."

"Riddles aren't supposed to be fair. Only true. You're the one who wasn't fair."

"I was right. The answer to a riddle only has to be right." He stalked a few paces away on the sand, hump swaying, knobbly knees knocking.

"You've offended him."

The Sphinx looked down her broken nose. *"It's hardly*

THE SPHINX AT DAWN

possible to speak to a camel without offending it. And he had no right to know the answer to that."

"But then you'd have had to eat me."

The Sphinx raised its massive stone wings and settled them again. *"All right, tell me. Tell me how he knew."*

"He's an old camel," the child said. "He has many friends and a long memory."

"Can he remember things that haven't been yet?"

"One of our friends is a unicorn. He moves through the years as easily as the camel moves across the desert." The boy stood still, listening, waiting.

In the far, far distance beyond the horizon, came the sound of silver on glass, and a paleness at the edge of the sky, cooler than the sun which glimmered gold below the curve of earth. Against the paleness came a sensation of motion; the desert floor vibrated with it; there was a tremor in the sand under the boy's feet; the ripples of the dunes curved and spread out in delicate waves. The motion against the horizon quivered; there was a brilliant sparking of desert dust, and then the sound and light receded.

"He won't always come. He's very shy."

"And I have had it made very clear to me that I am not fit companion for a unicorn." But she looked with satisfaction at the child. *"So you will be a very great king, then. I knew it! But I do not see why your friend the unicorn would bother*

with a camel. Camels are dirty, ignorant, and self-centered. I've never known one who wasn't. And always hungry and thirsty. I cannot see why they have the reputation they do for absten-tion when I go centuries without a single soul to eat. I am very hungry, young king."

"You have asked your riddles, and he has answered them."

"It wasn't fair—"

"Truth is not always fair, Sphinx," said the camel, "as you well know. He has answered the riddles and in doing so he has become a man and he will no longer be able to speak easily with us, his desert friends. We are going now. Farewell."

"Wait! I haven't tried him in history. Let me see if he knows any history."

"No Egyptian history then. Nothing peculiar out of the future or an unknown world."

"Why would I bother? You'd just tell him. No, I shall ask him his own history. That is something you know nothing about."

"I am uneasy. I don't like this. I—"

"No." The Sphinx gave a terrible smile. *"His history is where time and eternity touch, and you and your friends move only on one side or the other, not where they meet. Who, boy, was betrayed by a kiss?"* Her voice was intolerably gentle.

There was silence across the desert, and then a cold dawn wind, and across the wind blew a butterfly and landed briefly on the child's shoulder, then was blown along with the wind. "Why am I afraid? I know the answer to that. My father has told me much about the prophets. The answer to that question, Sphinx, is in the book of the prophet Samuel, and it refers to Joab, who kissed Amasa, and then killed him with a knife. Why am I afraid?"

"Because it is time to say goodbye. Because here in the desert you have made time and eternity meet, and you have answered the riddles. Now you must return to your own country and discover the kingdom of which you are the prince."

"You frighten me. I am only an ordinary boy and I do not think I want to be a prince."

"All boys want to be princes."

"But that is only in their dreams."

"There are visions which are so terrible that they become true. Let us say goodbye to the Sphinx. It is time to leave."

The boy raised his arm in farewell. He looked taller, not as much a child as when he had first ridden to the Sphinx across the desert.

"Come on, then, it's time for us to go. Your mother and father will be wondering where you are, and they'll be annoyed with me for bringing you home late when they are packing up and getting ready to leave. They'll never understand that you're safe as long as you're with me."

More or less. You can protect him from bandits and coca-trices with no respect for princes, and you find oases if it gets too hot. But you could not have kept me from eating him if I had wished to." She stretched out her enormous lethal claws, then sheathed them. "*But we have shared each other's words, little son, and we are part of one another now. Wherever you go from now on you will always take with you some of my wisdom and some of my indignation and some of my pain.*"

"Is there another riddle?"

"*Yes, there is the final riddle. What do you have that I will keep forever and ever and beyond the time my stone has crumbled into sand and beyond that again?*"

The boy ran quickly to the Sphinx and rubbed his hand lightly against her stone flank, then clambered up her side, panting, reaching for toe and finger holds, until he had reached her great head. "This is what you will keep," he said, and gave her a kiss. "You will keep my love."

"*That is always your answer, isn't it? The most difficult answer of all.*"

The boy scrambled down the Sphinx's side, gave a leap, and bounded onto the sand.

The sun lifted above the horizon, and Sphinx, camel, and child turned to gold.

"Come on. I shall have to run all the way in the heat." The camel knelt by the boy, who climbed up on the hump and took up the reins. He raised his hand once more to the Sphinx in salute.

The camel turned and began to gallop across the desert, rocking wildly, so that the boy had to hang on tightly to keep from falling off and could not see the shadow moving across the stone body of the Sphinx.

The Sphinx lay crouched, immobile, lifeless and inert stone. Her vacant eyes did not know the camel and the boy as they disappeared over the horizon.

ABOUT THE AUTHOR

Madeleine L'Engle (1918–2007) was an American author of more than sixty books, including novels for children and adults, poetry, and religious meditations. Her best-known work, *A Wrinkle in Time*, one of the most beloved young adult books of the twentieth century and a Newbery Medal winner, has sold more than fourteen million copies since its publication in 1962. Her other novels include *A Wind in the Door*, *A Swiftly Tilting Planet*, and *A Ring of Endless Light*. Born in New York City, L'Engle graduated from Smith College and worked in theater, where she met her husband, actor Hugh Franklin. L'Engle documented her marriage and family life in the four-book autobiographical series, the Crosswicks Journals. She also served as librarian and writer-in-residence at the Cathedral Church of Saint John the Divine in Manhattan for more than thirty years.

MADELEINE L'ENGLE

FROM OPEN ROAD MEDIA

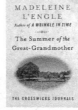

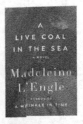

OPEN ROAD

INTEGRATED MEDIA

OPEN ROAD

INTEGRATED MEDIA

CPSIA information can be obtained
at www.ICGtesting.com
Printed in the USA
BVOW08s1435150418
513436BV00001B/129/P